Marzipan

1 cup almond paste (8-oz. can)
2 unbeaten egg whites
½ teaspoon vanilla
3 cups powdered sugar
food coloring

Crumble almond paste into small pieces. Stir in egg whites and vanilla using a mixer or spoon. Gradually add in sugar. Knead until smooth.

To make marzipan fruits and vegetables, divide dough into 4 or 5 pieces, depending on the number of colors desired. Knead food coloring into the dough one drop at a time. Model fruits and vegetables on a board lightly dusted with powdered sugar. Begin each piece by rolling a 1-inch ball. Whole cloves or bits of cinnamon stick make realistic stems. Roll lemons and oranges on a grater to achieve the rough-rind appearance.

You can add a blush of color by mixing food coloring, one drop at a time, with a few drops of water, and applying it with a small artist's brush. To glaze marzipan fruits and vegetables, mix ½ cup water with ½ cup corn syrup, and heat to boiling. Brush over entire piece with a small artist's brush. Store unused marzipan in a tightly covered container in the refrigerator.

SOFIE'S ROLE

Story by Amy Heath

Pictures by Sheila Hamanaka

Four Winds Press ❈ New York

Maxwell Macmillan Canada Toronto
Maxwell Macmillan International
New York Oxford Singapore Sydney

Four Winds Press, Macmillan Publishing Company, 866 Third Avenue, New York, NY 10022. Maxwell Macmillan Canada, Inc., 1200 Eglinton Avenue East, Suite 200, Don Mills, Ontario M3C 3N1. Macmillan Publishing Company is part of the Maxwell Communication Group of Companies. First edition. Printed and bound in the United States of America. 10 9 8 7 6 5 4 3 2 1 The text of this book is set in Hampshire Old Style. The illustrations are in oil on canvas. Typography by Christy Hale. Library of Congress Cataloging-in-Publication Data Heath, Amy. Sofie's role / story by Amy Heath ; pictures by Sheila Hamanaka.—1st ed., 1st American ed. p. cm. Summary: On the day before Christmas, Sofie makes her big debut serving customers in her family's busy bakery. ISBN 0-02-743505-9 [1. Bakers and bakeries—Fiction. 2. Family life—Fiction. 3. Christmas—Fiction.] I. Hamanaka, Sheila, ill. II. Title. PZ7.H3468So 1992 [E]—dc20 91-33488

Permission to reprint copyrighted material is gratefully acknowledged to the following: Wilton Enterprises, for the recipe for marzipan from The Wilton Way to Decorate for Christmas, copyright © 1976 by Wilton Enterprises, Chicago. David White, Inc., for the recipe for cinnamon stars from A World of Baking by Dolores Casella, copyright © 1968 by Dolores Casella.

*For Charlie, Julia Rose, and EmmaH, and all
who have worked at the B.P.S.*   —A.H.

*To my father, Conrad Yama,
a great connoisseur of roles*
      —S.H.

I snuggled between my parents in the frosty, dark car. Mama said I could help behind the counter at our bakery. If I wanted. She needed lots of help the day before Christmas.

I skated behind her on the slippery tile floor, past Rolf
punching dough-mounds and slapping them down in
a cloud of flour, s l a p . . . w h i s h ,

past the giant mixer
g a l u m p i n g round and round,
past the humming dragon-oven.
M m m m ! It breathed bread.

I peered into the sleeping shop.
I usually work with Papa, in the back.
But I will help out here this year.
Mama called it my "big debut."

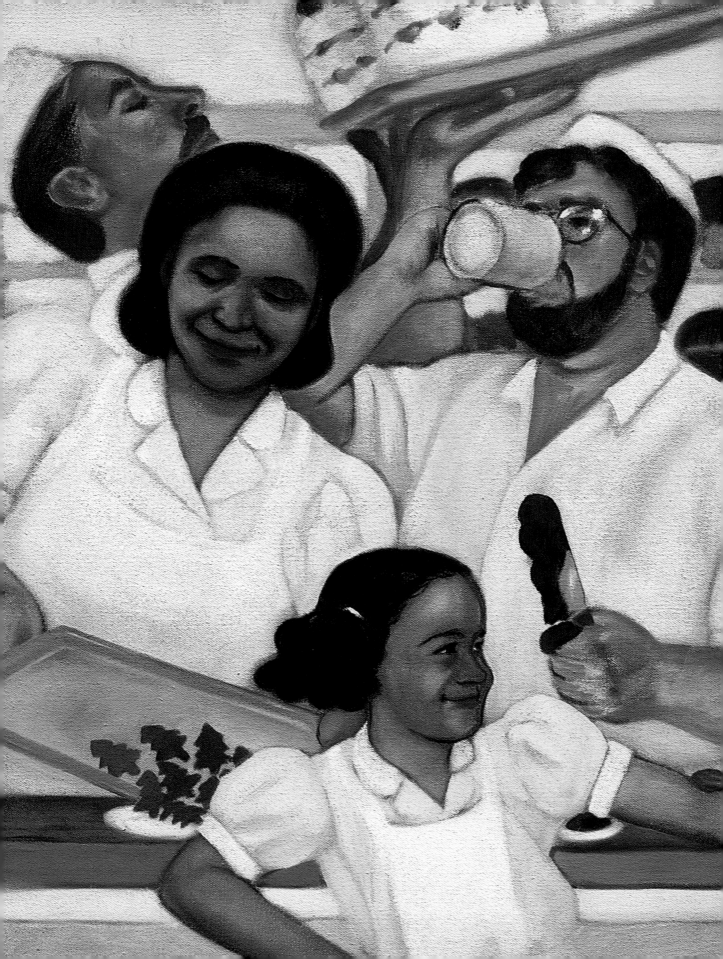

I helped her make tea. We fixed hard rolls
with cheese and apple slices.
But no one sat down to eat breakfast!
Papa frosted Yule log cakes. Nibble. Sip.
Mama slid kuchen onto cardboard plates.
Nibble. Sip.
Danny boxed deliveries. Nibble. Sip.
I practiced my lines for out front. "May I help you?
Who's next, please?" Gobble. Gulp.
The three college students came. "I'm going
to work out front today," I told them.
"All *right!*" they said.

In quiet light we set the stage. We filled the cases
with kuchen and tortes, with gingerbread houses
and gingerbread sleighs. We heaped golden trays
with dominosteine and six-pointed cinnamon stars.

I folded a tower of boxes.
   Mama slipped across a sea
of bread crumbs. She almost dropped
a whole pan of Black Forest slices.
   "There's your sweeping cue, Sofie,"
Mama said.
   I swept the floor.

I peeked through the window-case curtains
for one last look at the gingerbread village
with its marzipan market.

But I quickly pulled my head back in.
A mass of wool-wrapped giants
pressed against the window.

"Places, everyone!" Mama called. "Almost curtain time!"
My throat got tight.
My tongue felt dry.
I looked into the back.

Papa saw me.
He winked and raised his cup of tea.
Mama snapped the shop lights on.
She opened the curtains and unlocked the door.

The bell over the door jingled wildly.
The floor rumbled under all those boots.

"May I help someone?" Mama called loudly.
"Who's next?" one of the students shouted.
"Was that one or two pounds assorted?" said another.
"One stollen and this poppyseed roll."
"I'm next!"
"Two pounds. No pfeffernuss!"
I squeaked, "May I help you?"
Nobody heard me.
I swallowed and tried again. "Who's next, please?"
Nothing happened. I need water, I thought.

Cinnamon Stars

¾ cup egg whites
1 pound superfine granulated sugar
  or sifted powdered sugar
1 tablespoon cinnamon
1 teaspoon grated lemon rind
1 pound grated unblanched almonds
sugar
flour

Beat the egg whites until they form stiff peaks. Gradually beat in the sugar and then the cinnamon and lemon rind. Beat in the grated almonds last. Dust a breadboard or pastry canvas with a mixture of equal parts of sugar and flour. Working with a small portion of dough at a time, pat it out to a thickness of ⅜ inch. Cut with a cooky cutter, or cut into squares or oblongs. Place on lightly buttered cooky sheets and bake in the oven at 275° about 25 to 30 minutes. Makes about 4 dozen cookies.

I slipped around to the back. The phone rang.
Mama and the others were zipping around,
waiting on customers...*Brrr-ING!*
Papa was up to his elbows in buttercream frosting...
Brrr-ING!
Danny was loading the truck...*Brrr-ING!*
Rolf never answers the phone...*Brrr—*

"Merry Christmas. Broadway Pastries," I answered.
I scribbled an order for an apricot kuchen and a
Yule log cake.

The phone rang again and again. I took more orders,
described Papa's linzer torte, and told people we would be
closing at three o'clock.

I bagged loaves of rye with seeds and packed a pound of almond macaroons.

I was so busy I didn't notice the crowd disappear from the shop.

As I put the last order on the order shelf, a girl from my school came in.

Mama was in the back. The college students were packing cookies.

"Hi!" I said. "Merry Christmas. May I help you?"

My voice didn't squeak!

"Hi!" she smiled. "How much is a gingerbread sleigh?"

"Two twenty-five."

"How many cinnamon stars would fit into it, do you think?" she asked eagerly. "We're three in my family. It's for a present."

I put the sleigh on the counter and arranged three star cookies. They fit perfectly.

The girl's freckles danced when she smiled. I smiled, too.

While I carefully packed it all in a box she said,
"Is it hard working back there?"

I centered the "Broadway Pastries" label on the lid and
taped it closed.

I looked up at her. "It's a piece of cake!" I said.